MR. T SAYS:

"The blessed of us must save the less of us."

"I don't worry. I don't doubt. I'm daring. I'm a rebel."

"If they didn't love me before, they can't love me now."

"There are too many dream-killers in the world. Don't let anybody tell you that you can't be somebody."

"It takes a smart man to play dumb."

"Any man who doesn't love his mama can't be no friend of mine."

And much more. . . .

TOUGH & TENDER

The Story of
MR. T
by Veronica Michael

TOUGH
AND
TENDER
The Story of
Mr. T

Veronica Michael

A SIGNET BOOK

NEW AMERICAN LIBRARY

NAL BOOKS ARE AVAILABLE AT QUANTITY DISCOUNTS
WHEN USED TO PROMOTE PRODUCTS OR SERVICES.
FOR INFORMATION PLEASE WRITE TO PREMIUM MARKETING DIVISION.
NEW AMERICAN LIBRARY. 1633 BROADWAY.
NEW YORK. NEW YORK 10019.

Copyright © 1984 by Veronica Bennett

Special thanks to Barbara Walters, who so graciously allowed use of material from her interview with Mr. T conducted on November 11, 1983.

SIGNET, SIGNET CLASSIC, MENTOR, PLUME, MERIDIAN AND NAL BOOKS
are published by New American Library,
1633 Broadway, New York, New York 10019

First Printing, November 1984

1 2 3 4 5 6 7 8 9

PRINTED IN THE UNITED STATES OF AMERICA

Chapter 1

▼▼▼▼▼▼▼▼▼▼▼▼▼▼▼▼▼▼▼▼▼▼▼▼▼▼▼▼▼▼▼

What Mr. T Is *Really* Like

"You're dead meat!" When Mr. T snarls that familiar line on *The A Team*, everyone knows that the bad guy is doomed. "Pity the fool," because when Mr. T is ma-a-a-d, he's ba-a-a-d and the villain always ends up very sa-a-a-d that he tangled with Mr. T. His bulging biceps and massive chest, that power-packed swagger and terrifying scowl can and do turn grown men into puddles of quivering jelly, on screen and off.

Is Mr. T really so mean? "If I were, you couldn't pay kids to get near me." And nobody is paying the forty-two million fans who watch his television shows every week. No one is bribing kids who mob Mr. T at the schools, shopping centers and hospitals he visits when he is not filming *The A Team*.

Rev. Henry Hardy, the pastor of Mr. T's church in Chicago, Illinois, says that Mr. T is nothing like his rough, tough television image. "He is very sensitive and concerned . . . very religious and spiritual—and humble."

Is Mr. T really as mean as he looks?

"I'm a tough guy with a big heart," says Mr. T. "If I didn't look so tough, nobody would pay attention to me." And Mr. T wants people to pay attention to him because the most important thing in his life is

Mr. T with a couple of his adoring
fans.

the message he has for kids: "Believe in God and
yourself, no matter who you are. Everybody wants
success, but only a few are willing to work for it. I
say, study long enough and hard enough and you'll
succeed."

A lot of men who are as big and strong as Mr. T
is, or who are as rich and famous, might start to
think that they are better than other people. But not
Mr. T. "Without religion I never could have become
a star." And he really means it.

True to his religious beliefs, Mr. T lives simply.
His home is an apartment in a high-rise building in
Los Angeles, California. It is nothing like the big,
fancy houses with swimming pools, guard dogs and

Well, he's not playing a violin, but Mr. T can sure get down and get into the mood.

▼▼▼▼▼▼▼▼▼▼▼▼▼▼▼▼▼▼▼▼▼▼▼▼▼▼▼

tennis courts of some other television stars. Mr. T's apartment is small and quiet. It's where he goes to relax after putting in long hours stomping out crime on *The A Team.*

He lives by himself, and he says that he spends a lot of time at home alone. He doesn't like the glitzy Hollywood nightlife. "When I went to parties, they said, 'Come on, Mr. T, make a muscle' . . . So I stopped going. I refuse to be a token. I'm no uncle T." When Mr. T does go out, he tools around town in a classic old Rolls-Royce automobile. And he's always ready to pose for photographs with fans who are lucky enough to have a camera in their back pocket if they bump into Mr. T at the local hamburger stand.

If this spread isn't enough to fill up Mr. T, he can stop by McDonald's for a few Quarterpounders on the way home.

▼▼▼▼▼▼▼▼▼▼▼▼▼▼▼▼▼▼▼▼▼▼▼▼▼▼▼▼▼▼▼▼▼▼▼▼

His favorite television show is *The Beverly Hillbillies* because, as he says, "they are humble, God-fearing folk; they aren't trying to impress anyone."

In his spare time, Mr. T often reads the Bible and other religious books. His other favorite stories are about great men who had to struggle to reach their goals in life—men like scientist Albert Einstein, inventor Henry Ford and President Abraham Lincoln. Mr. T listens to music, too. He'd like to learn to play the violin because, he says, "that's the sweetest music in the world."

People who work on television shows often have to get up before daylight because it takes so long for makeup, costumes, lighting and rehearsals before they get down to the actual business of filming the story. Those long workdays eat into Mr. T's sleep hours, and he's a man who likes his sack time. Early to bed and late to rise is how Mr. T likes to live. But don't think he's lazy. Every day he works out on his own set of weights and barbells. Then he rips into

9

one hundred—count them!—one hundred pushups and one hundred situps to keep those humongous muscles in tip-top condition.

Mr. T is five feet, eleven inches tall and he weighs about two hundred and twenty pounds. It takes a lot of food to fill up a body that big and when Mr. T is hungry—get out of his way!

In a restaurant, a *Washington Post* reporter overheard Mr. T tell the waiter, "If I don't get enough to eat, I'll break a table in half." Then he started off with two pieces of chocolate cake, followed by two steaks, two baked potatoes, three bowls of rice and another dessert. Sometimes breakfast is a whole box of Cheerios with four bananas. And when he goes to McDonald's, Mr. T has been known to put away three Quarterpounders with cheese, a strawberry milkshake and two large orders of french fries. So, don't ask Mr. T to dinner without laying in heavy supplies!

Mr. T doesn't smoke and he never drinks any kind of alcohol. He won't touch coffee or cola drinks either because they contain caffeine and Mr. T believes caffeine is harmful to his body.

A lot of people don't know that Mr. T has a daughter. Her name is Lisa. She was born on February 11, 1971, and she lives in Chicago with her mother, Phyllis. Mr. T takes his responsibility as a father seriously. From the very beginning he sent money to Phyllis and Lisa, even when it meant he had to make do with less for himself. Now that he's making megabucks, he can give them much more.

Mr. T telephones Lisa several times a week from Los Angeles and when he goes home to Chicago sometimes he picks her up in a limousine and sweeps her away on shopping sprees to Chicago's fancy stores.

Mr. T and one of his "tots" eye one another with mutual delight.

▼▼▼

Lisa never misses *The A Team* on television and Mr. T has flown her out to visit him in Los Angeles several times. He takes her to the studio where *The A Team* is filmed so that she can see how the show is made and meet the other stars.

All children are special to Mr. T. He keeps a box of photographs that fans have sent him from all over the world. He likes to call his fans "Mr. T's Tots" and he says that "if Jerry Lewis can have his kids, if Charlie can have his Angels, why can't Mr. T have his tots?"

"Kids listen to me," says Mr. T, "not because they fear me, but because they look up to me." And they look up to him because he takes no guff from anybody. There is nothing wishy-washy about Mr.

T. He lives by the rules and whining excuses for bad behavior get nowhere with him. He may be a marshmallow when it comes to little kids, but he's no pushover. Anyone who gets out of line around him will find out just how fast Mr. T can turn fierce and angry.

Maybe his astrological sign, Gemini, which represents the twins, explains the two sides of Mr. T. He's a tough guy, for sure, but he's never been afraid to show his soft side. Mr. T says he used to cry himself to sleep at night when he was trying to get started in life and couldn't find a job. He cried when a little boy he knew, who was only eight years old, died of cancer. And even now, his eyes water when he talks about how hard his mother struggled to raise her twelve children with dignity and the feeling that they could grow up to be *somebody*.

Mr. T owns a million dollars worth of gold now. He is a superhero to children all over the world. But he didn't start out that way. "I was born in poverty," he says, "and came from a broken home. Millions in that situation turn to drugs. I didn't. I looked to the sky."

FACTS AND FIGURES AND FAVORITES

REAL NAME:	Lawrence Tureaud
BIRTHPLACE:	Chicago, Illinois
BIRTHDATE:	May 21, 1952
ASTROLOGICAL SIGN:	Gemini, the twins
HEIGHT:	5' 11"
WEIGHT:	220 pounds
HAIR:	Black
EYES:	Brown
RELIGION:	Born-again Christian
FAMILY:	7 brothers 4 sisters
DAUGHTER:	Lisa. Born February 11, 1971
INCOME:	Over $3,000,000 a year
WORTH OF JEWELRY:	Over $1,000,000
FAVORITE TV SHOW:	*The Beverly Hillbillies*
FAVORITE MUSIC:	Anything played on the violin
GOAL IN LIFE:	To become a full-time preacher
MOTTO:	Tough and Tender
MESSAGE:	Be Somebody!
WHERE TO WRITE TO MR. T:	*The A Team* Fan Club 7083 Hollywood Boulevard Hollywood, California 90028

Chapter 2

▾▾▾▾▾▾▾▾▾▾▾▾▾▾▾▾▾▾▾▾▾▾▾▾▾▾▾▾▾▾▾▾▾▾▾▾▾

Growing Up

Mr. T was born on May 21, 1952. He was named Lawrence Tureaud but later his father changed the family name to Tero. There were already nine other children in the family before Mr. T was born and Mrs. Tero had two more after that. So counting Mr. T, there are twelve kids in the family.

They lived in the South Side of Chicago, Illinois, one of the poorest sections of any city in America. For many years, the whole family lived jammed together in a tiny apartment. "We were poor," Mr. T says, "but we smiled."

Because he was the youngest boy, Mr. T's family called him "Little Man," but not for long. His older brothers were all wrestlers and boxers in school and Little Man got the benefit of their experience. They taught him to do situps, pushups and jumping jacks. Every day they put him through exercises to develop his muscles and become as strong as the other men in the Tero family.

Mr. T was rowdy as a kid, getting into plenty of

fights. Whenever he came home bruised and beaten, he'd get another whipping from his mother. More than once he was suspended from school for fighting. Somehow, he made it through childhood without any lasting damage, probably thanks to his brothers' training.

Mr. T's mother couldn't afford to buy a television set, so the kids had to play games like Monopoly. At Christmas, the family didn't have enough money for presents, but everyone loved each other and that made it easier to do without the things that other children had.

Mr. T never had brand-new clothes of his own—only hand-me-downs from his older brothers. They were so poor that sometimes there wasn't even enough food. Mr. T jokes that all they had to eat were "oatmeal, no meal and miss a meal." He made up a poem about it that he recited for Barbara Walters when she interviewed Mr. T for her television special:

" 'Twas the night before Christmas and all through
   the pad,
Gravy and biscuits was all that we had.
The stockings were hung by the chimney with
   care,
Hoping the welfare check soon would be there.

Mrs. Tero worked as a maid for white people in a better part of town. Mr. Tero was a junkman and sometimes he worked as a delivery truck driver—when he could find a job at all. Keeping twelve kids clothed and fed was a never-ending problem of juggling what little money they had.

When Mr. T was only five years old, his father

moved out. Although Mr. T was too young to understand why his dad left—for welfare reasons—Mrs. Tero never let her children forget how much their father loved them. Now that Mr. T is grown up, he doesn't have any bad feelings about what his father did. He understands. "If somebody thinks for one moment I don't love my father, or that I disrespect him in any way," he warns, "I'll personally find him and break every bone in his body."

Sometimes Mr. T's mother had to borrow money from the neighbors until the next welfare check arrived. But she always paid it back. And instead of taking a bus to report to the welfare office, Mrs. Tero saved a few cents by walking. Mr. T remembers seeing her trudging through snowstorms in Chicago's cold, windy winters with only a thin, raggedy old coat to keep her warm.

Mr. T admits that he stole to help out. "I haven't done anything I'm ashamed of. I stole to survive. I stole food. Never snatched anybody's purse," he says. "Nothing like that." He took bread from the bakery and milk from the dairy. He says he once took three bags of groceries home in a supermarket cart. He told his mother he had earned the money for the food cleaning a man's garage. He lied because he knew that if his mother found out he had stolen the food, she wouldn't touch it. Now Mr. T is sorry he lied, even if it was about food the family needed. He believes that lying is a shameful thing to do, especially to your mother. He "would rather die in burning hell than dishonor and disrespect my mother."

Three of Mr. T's older brothers dropped out of school because the family needed money so badly. One of them went into the Army. Another joined the Marines and the third found a job. All of them sent money home and that helped ease some of the money pressures.

Mr. T is thankful for the sacrifices that his family made so that he, the baby boy of the family, could finish school. Now that he has so much money, Mr. T helps support his parents and all his brothers and sisters. "If my mother could take care of us on $87.00 a month, surely I can take care of my family on the millions I make," he says.

Mr. T adores his mother and he phones her every week from Los Angeles. "She could have left," he says, but "she kept us together. Otherwise we'd all probably be strung out on drugs. Or in gangs. They were all around."

Believe it or not, Mr. T doesn't have any regrets about not having had a bicycle or store-bought clothes or a television set when he was a kid, "because the poverty made me what I am. If I had to do it all over again, I'd take it the same way."

He says that he has always liked the rougher side of life and that if he hadn't had sports to let off steam, he might have turned to drugs or worse. At Dunbar Vocational High School, Mr. T put all his excess energy into sports.

He loved wrestling and practiced for hours and hours every day. He was called "Tero the Terrible" and won scads of trophies and medals in wrestling matches. He was so good that he held the City Wrestling Championship for two straight years and he represented his school against other wrestlers from all over the state of Illinois.

Mr. T also played football during all four years of high school. By his second year he was playing on the varsity squad. As team captain, he led his school

Mr. T replays his football-hero days.

▼▼▼▼▼▼▼▼▼▼▼▼▼▼▼▼▼▼▼▼▼▼▼▼▼▼

to victory during his senior year in the big game against Dunbar's archrival.

It is common for many people to think that athletes are dumb. That idea made Mr. T angry and we know that when Mr. T is angry, something terrible is going to happen. But he knew that this was not a problem he could fix with his fists. Instead Mr. T made sure he did well in school. Nobody was able to say that Mr. T was just another dumb jock. By the time Mr. T was ready for college, he had excellent marks and an outstanding football record. He was offered scholarships to more than thirty schools, including members of the Big Ten and Ivy League. He chose a small, all-black college in Texas called Prairie View A & M because he liked their football team.

Mr. T spells out his message—be somebody—to an audience of kids on the television show *A.M. Chicago*.

▼▼▼▼▼▼▼▼▼▼▼▼▼▼▼▼▼▼▼▼▼▼▼▼▼▼▼▼▼▼▼▼▼▼▼▼▼▼▼

There, in the fall of 1969, Mr. T became a star football player. He was so popular with his classmates that they elected him president of the freshman class. And he still kept up his marks. That first year Mr. T made the honor roll with a four-point grade average—six A's. But he didn't return to Prairie View after that first year.

In the early 1970s, a lot of people, including college students, were demonstrating their beliefs, and one night in February, 1970, a riot broke out at Mr. T's school. People smashed windows, broke into buildings and looted campus stores. Fires blazed in dormitories. Mr. T says that he wasn't there that night. But later, in the confusion of trying to sort out who had done what, Mr. T was accused, along with many other students, of taking part in the riot. He tried to prove he hadn't been there, but he was suspended from school anyway.

Back home in Chicago, Mr. T had to figure out what to do to earn a living. He's so famous now that anybody would hire him. But in 1970, Mr. T was just another poor, young, black kid. Mrs. Tero had taught Mr. T that if he tried hard and believed in himself, he could grow up to be somebody. Now he had to prove it.

Chapter 3

▼▼▼▼▼▼▼▼▼▼▼▼▼▼▼▼▼▼▼▼▼▼▼▼▼▼▼▼▼▼▼▼▼▼▼

Trying to Be Somebody

Some people seem to be born knowing what they want to be when they grow up. From the time they are very little kids they talk about becoming a doctor or a teacher or a soldier or a writer or whatever. Then they just grow up and do it. But they are the exceptions. It takes most people a long time to find out what they want to be and they have to try several kinds of jobs before they find the one they like. Mr. T was like that. He knew he wanted to *be somebody*, but he didn't know exactly what.

Mr. T answered newspaper ads, filled out forms and went on interviews. It took a long time before he finally got a job as a house man in a hotel. He had to set up chairs and tables for people who rented meeting rooms and then put everything away afterwards. After a few months, he quit the hotel to take a job as a night janitor in a bank. At the same time he worked during the day as a security guard in another bank, and later on, at a hospital.

In 1972, Mr. T was hired as a gym teacher at a

special school in Chicago that took only the worst kids from all over the city: teenage boys who were slow learners, or wouldn't go to school at all, or couldn't stop fighting with kids and teachers. Mr. T knew the problems his students had at home—not enough food to eat, not enough clothes to wear, crime all around them. And he knew that they had to be tough to survive. So he was tough on them. No nonsense at all, or they had Mr. T to answer to. He had to knock a few heads together, but the boys came to respect Mr. T and even love him. He was the only father or brother some of them knew. Mr. T says working with those kids changed his life. Nothing else Mr. T has done before or since has ever made him feel as good as helping those boys.

After three years, the school ran out of money and had to be closed. But Mr. T feels it was a success anyway because so many of the kids learned that if they wanted to live differently, they could. It was up to them.

Mr. T had always liked the idea of protecting people from harm and he thought that a great way of doing that would be to become a bodyguard. He knew he needed more experience than guarding banks and hospitals, so in 1975, he joined the National Guard as a military policeman. The drill instructors worked twenty pounds off Mr. T's body and kept him busy from early morning to late at night. The training was tough, but Mr. T shaped up as one of the best. When he returned to Chicago, he picked up another security guard job and set himself up in his own part-time business as a personal bodyguard.

He called himself "The World's Greatest Bodyguard." He says that he may not have been the

Mr. T reunited with one of his bodyguarding clients, singer Donna Summer.

"roughest, toughest, baddest, ugliest or meanest" bodyguard, but there was no one any better. The business cards he handed out were printed with the saying, "Next to God, there is no better protection than I." He wasn't kidding.

Mr. T dedicated his life to the people who hired him. "I'm willing to die for a client," he says. "I get hit with all kinds of things when I'm bodyguarding. If a guy has a gun, I'm the one who will get shot."

Even though Mr. T knew that he could be killed

bodyguarding people, he never liked to carry a gun. "What can a gun do?" he asks. "Can a gun stop sickle cell anemia? Can it stop a heart attack?" He accepted the fact that bodyguarding was dangerous and he took pride in relying on his size and strength to do the job. "There's something special about bodyguarding. I figured if bodyguarding was too rough for me, I would have become a baker or a cook or a secretary. There's something about the danger. I thrive on it."

Mr. T was bodyguard to some of the most famous people in the world—singers Donna Summer, Diana Ross and Michael Jackson, Presidential candidate Jesse Jackson and even championship boxers like Leon Spinks and The Greatest himself, Muhammad Ali.

Mr. T charged big bucks for his protection services because he was the best and, no doubt the biggest, bodyguard around. Even before people knew how good he was, Mr. T was paid several hundred dollars a day. When word got out that no one else was as fearless as Mr. T, he could charge even more money. His last bodyguarding fee was $10,000 a day.

Mr. T didn't protect just rich people, though. Mr. T believes that everybody needs a bodyguard at least once in a while and that is why he bodyguarded "regular people" too. "I bodyguarded welfare mothers," he says. "I bodyguarded people who couldn't afford my salary. Those are more important to me than the famous people." Bodyguarding gave Mr. T a great sense of respect for himself. Getting a client home safe and sound "means more to me than all the money he can pay me because I feel my self-worth there. I'm saving a life."

Famous people need bodyguards because sometimes fans can get over-excited. When crowds of people are pushing and shoving, it is easy for someone to be crushed or trampled. Now that Mr. T is famous, even he needs bodyguards. Two of his brothers who are just as beefy and brawny as he is, always travel with Mr. T. Mr. T can take time to talk with kids and sign autographs without worrying that someone will be hurt in the jostling and commotion around him.

Mr. T worked as a bodyguard off and on for about six years. During that time he also worked as a bouncer at night in a disco called Dingbats. His job was to check people's ages at the door to be sure they were old enough to be let into the club. He also had to be tough enough to take on guys who might have had too much to drink.

It was while he was working at Dingbats, in 1980, that Mr. T was asked to appear on television in "The Toughest Bouncer in America" contest. He was up against some of the heftiest guys in the country, but Mr. T made mincemeat of them. He won the contest and was asked back to defend his title a couple of months later. He won the contest again and this time a very famous movie star was watching.

When Sylvester Stallone saw Mr. T smash through a door six inches thick and then saw him throw a 115-pound man eighteen feet across a room, he knew this bruiser was a man he needed to know.

Sylvester Stallone was looking for someone to play Clubber Lang, the man Rocky had to fight to regain his boxing title in the movie, *Rocky III*. Mr. T auditioned and won the part over 1,500 other men who tried out.

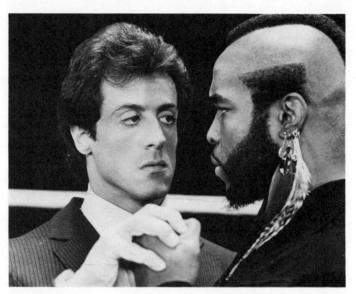

Mr. T and Sylvester Stallone squared off eye-to-eye before filming began for *Rocky III*.

▼▼▼

Being big and tough and strong enough to protect people or win street fights isn't the same as being a good boxer. It takes very special training, and Mr. T had to take boxing lessons before they could film the fight scenes for the movie. Sylvester Stallone told Mr. T that they were not going to just pretend to hit each other in the movie because the people in the audience can tell when actors pull their punches. Stallone wanted the fights to be as real as they could possibly be without causing any terrible injury. Mr. T trained for three months and he looked great on the screen when the movie was finished. But he admits that Sylvester Stallone was still the better fighter. Rocky clobbered Clubber. "Man, he really punished me," says Mr. T. "He hurt me more times than I care to remember."

Acting came easy to Mr. T. "I knew I could act a long time ago when I was in first grade," he says. "Teachers used to tell me 'why don't you stop acting a fool, stop acting a clown.' So I knew if I could act a fool, act a clown, I could act anything." Sylvester Stallone "just told me to be myself. I didn't take any acting lessons." The audiences thought Mr. T was terrific and the movie was a smashing success. Mr. T was finally somebody, and it wasn't long before he was starring in his own television series.

Chapter 4

▼▼▼▼▼▼▼▼▼▼▼▼▼▼▼▼▼▼▼▼▼▼▼▼▼▼▼▼▼▼▼▼▼▼▼▼▼▼

The A Team
and Beyond

Bullet holes puncture a blood-red television screen—a voice announces, "If you have a problem, if no one else can help and if you can find them, maybe *you* can hire—*The A Team*." When you hear those words, it has to be Tuesday night at eight o'clock and time for the hottest show on NBC-TV. Forty-two million people tune in each week to watch the roughest, toughest four men alive fight to protect the innocent, punish the guilty and defend justice.

As the story goes, four Vietnam veterans were sent to prison by military police for a crime they did not commit. They escaped, returned to Los Angeles and now they hire themselves out for dangerous missions that no one else has the guts to try. They need to earn enough money to pay a lawyer to take their case and prove their innocence. But until they do, they must fight off not only the villains, but also Colonel Decker and the rest of the military police who are still chasing them.

John "Hannibal" Smith is the cigar-twirling leader

The *A Team*: Mr. T, "Howling Mad"
Murdock, Templeton "Face" Peck and
in front, John "Hannibal" Smith.

▼▼▼▼▼▼▼▼▼▼▼▼▼▼▼▼▼▼▼▼▼▼▼▼▼▼▼▼

of the team, each member of which has his own
special talent. Templeton "Face" Peck is so hand-
some and so clever that he can sucker anybody into
believing anything he says, no matter how strange
or silly it sounds. "Howling Mad" Murdock is their
ace airplane pilot. He will fly anything, big or small,
old or new. It doesn't matter to him what shape the
plane is in, he'll get it off the ground. He is also so
weird that none of the rest of the team can tell if he
is really crazy or not. Mr. T's character is named
B.A., for "Bad Attitude" Baracus. He is their A-one

Mr. T as B.A. Baracus gets tough
with "Howling Mad" Murdock.

▼▼▼▼▼▼▼▼▼▼▼▼▼▼▼▼▼▼▼▼▼▼▼▼

mechanic and the brute strength of *The A Team*.
But when he's not pounding the Wheaties out of
some poor fool, he works in a day-care center. "That's
not acting," says Mr. T. "There's no difference between B.A. and T." B.A. even wears the same haircut and the same gold chains and feather earrings as
Mr. T.

Mr. T won't let B.A. do anything on screen that
Mr. T wouldn't do in real life. Part of B.A.'s person-
ality on the show is his fear of flying. When *The A
Team* first began, the other members of the team
doped up B.A. when he had to get on an airplane.
Mr. T's mother told him that she didn't like to see
him taking drugs, even if it was just an act for a

television show. Mr. T agreed with her and he got the writers to change the script. Now when B.A. has to fly, the other team members find ways to trick him into getting on the airplane. Mr. T won't ever mess with his image. "You don't see me doing any beer commercials or smoking. I wouldn't play a drug addict or a pimp or a dope dealer or anything like that," he says.

Some people complain that The A Team is too violent, but Mr. T disagrees, "We fight but there's never blood." And he prays before he films a scene in which he punches out some dummy's lights. "When I be fighting or whatever on TV, it's all just fun, we don't hurt anybody. But I don't want you to be a fighter," he cautions kids. "Study to be a scientist, study to be an astronaut. Everyone can't be Mr. T."

The A Team is filmed in and around Los Angeles. It is a lot more complicated to make a television show than it looks on the screen. There are a hundred or more people behind the scenes. First the writers have to think up a story and prepare a script. The director decides where to put the cameras and he tells the actors exactly what to do and where to stand so that the cameras will find them. There are several cameras and each one has a cameraman to run it. A lighting director figures out where the different kinds of lights go and he has several people called gaffers and grips to help him put the lights in the right places. All the metal poles and rigging for the lights make the area around a scene look like a giant Erector Set.

The floor is a mess of twisted electrical cords and cables used to bring in the power to run all the cameras, lights and sound equipment. The audio *man* takes care of microphones and he checks to see that the actors' voices can be heard clearly.

There are *makeup artists* who do more than brush on lipstick, eye shadow and blusher. They have amazing boxes of bruises, scratches, cuts and bumps to paste on the actors who must look bashed and battered after a fight scene.

The *costume designer* creates the clothes the actors wear and the *wardrobe department* sews the costumes, keeps them clean and ironed and helps the actors zip up.

The *set designer* draws up the plans for the "sets," then he supervises the *carpenters* and *electricians* who build the sets. The *prop man* collects all the furniture, pictures, lamps, curtains and anything else needed to "dress" the set. Smaller things like books, guns or telephones are called properties or "props" and it is the prop man's job to make sure they are in the correct place so that when an actor has to pick up a gun, for instance, the gun is where he expects it to be.

Gophers are the lowliest members of the production crew and are usually young men and women working on their first jobs. They are called gophers because they have to "go for" coffee, sandwiches, a missing prop or anything else that someone needs in a hurry.

Stunt men and women have the most dangerous jobs. They wear costumes identical to the ones the characters they "stand in" for wear, and they take the places of the actors when the script calls for them to jump out of airplanes or fall off tall buildings or crash through plate-glass windows or drive cars at breakneck speeds. "Stunts" have to be carefully planned and rehearsed so that no one gets

Mr. T tiptoes through the tangle of equipment on the set of *The A Team*.

▼▼▼▼▼▼▼▼▼▼▼▼▼▼▼▼▼▼▼▼▼▼▼▼▼▼▼▼▼

hurt. Stunt people are brave and courageous experts who take daredevil chances to make TV shows like *The A Team* as exciting and spine-tingling as possible.

You can see that there is a lot of work to be done before everything is ready for the actors to go "on camera" to film the show. And actors often complain that the hardest part of their job is to "hurry up and wait"—and wait—and wait. Some of them read books, or they play games like checkers and chess, or maybe backgammon. It can be awfully boring to wait so long, and there is usually a lot of horseplay and silliness to help pass the time.

Marla Heasley, who played Tania on *The A Team* during the 1983/84 television season, says that Mr. T likes to tease people who don't know him well by

Aw, he isn't so tough.
▼▼▼▼▼▼▼▼▼▼▼▼▼▼▼▼▼▼▼▼▼▼▼▼▼▼▼▼▼▼▼

sounding gruff and mean. When a *TV Guide* reporter
visited the set in March 1984, Mr. T hollered out for
everyone to hear, "There's been a lot of rumors
about animosity on this set! Now tell me: anybody
who doesn't like anybody, tell me right now! Because," and he looked at the reporter with menace
in his eyes, "enquiring minds want to know!" He
was letting the reporter know that he didn't want
anything bad written about the show, even if there
had been gossip in other magazines. But Marla says
that Mr. T doesn't really mean it when he sounds

scary like that. He reminds her of a big brother heckling a little brother or sister.

Mr. T is friendly with all the people he works with. "I have a good relationship with all the guys," he says. "I think this set has more God than any set around."

The A Team is as much a blockbuster show in Europe as it is in America. When they visited Holland in the summer of 1984, Mr. T and the rest of the team found 25,000 screaming fans waiting to greet them at the airport when they arrived. And because he has become such a superstar, Mr. T was given another television show by NBC.

The Mr. T Show is a Saturday morning cartoon program. Mr. T plays the coach of a gymnastics team. The main members of the team are two boys named Jeff and Spike and two girls named Kim and Robin. When they are not practicing or performing on the parallel bars, the rings or the pommel horse, they get themselves into all kinds of hair-raising scrapes that Mr. T must rescue them from. And he does it in his usual macho-to-the-max style. "Just wait till I get my hands on you turkeys!" he told the kidnappers in one episode. "You'll be in pieces, chumps!"

At the end of each show, Mr. T comes on the screen in person to punch up the message behind the day's adventure. "Take it from me, someone who's been there," he tells everyone watching. "Take it from me, Mr. T." And who would dare do otherwise?

Making the cartoon show is a lot easier for Mr. T than filming *The A Team*. Artists draw the thousands of still pictures it takes to make a thirty-minute program. When that is done, Mr. T goes into

Mr. T daring anyone to make fun of his hula skirt. He was taping a TV special with Bob Hope in Hawaii.

▼▼▼▼▼▼▼▼▼▼▼▼▼▼▼

Gary Coleman, dressed as a tiny Mr. T, listens carefully to the real thing on an episode of *Diff'rent Strokes*.

▼▼▼▼▼▼▼▼▼▼▼▼▼▼

Moments after this photo was taken, Mr. T got dunked in the water on *Games People Play* on TV.

▼▼▼▼▼▼▼▼▼▼▼▼▼▼▼▼▼

Mr. T gets a lift from soap opera star Michael Damian when they both took part in a charity softball game.

▼▼▼▼▼▼▼▼▼▼▼▼▼▼▼▼▼▼▼

a recording studio to match his voice to the pictures on the screen. Filming his speech for the end of the show takes only a few minutes in the television studio.

Mr. T sometimes appears on other people's TV shows. He regularly competes against stars from other series on *Battle of the Network Stars*. He made a guest appearance on *Diff'rent Strokes* in 1983. Gary Coleman, who plays Arnold, wore a bunch of chains and a wig so that he looked just like a tiny Mr. T. Another time Mr. T did the dressing up when he wore a hula skirt in a show he taped in Hawaii with comedian Bob Hope.

Mr. T has made two other movies besides *Rocky III*. He played himself in a small part in *Penitentiary II*, in 1982. Then he had the starring role in *D.C. Cab*. "I play a struggling cab driver concerned about the kids on the street," he explained. "But no one will listen to me, because I'm not flashy like the pimp or the dope dealer. But then things change."

Mr. T has already filmed a TV movie for CBS called *The Toughest Man in the World* in which he plays Bruise Brubaker, a nightclub bouncer who works part-time in a youth club. Bruise saves the club from going under by competing in a muscleman contest.

There are sure to be more movies from Mr. T in the future. He says he would like to play uplifting roles, people like Moses, a disciple of Jesus or perhaps a great hero to mankind—someone who finds a cure for cancer, for example.

"I'm talented and flexible," he says. "I could play Hamlet even though I look like King Kong."

Chapter 5

▼▼▼▼▼▼▼▼▼▼▼▼▼▼▼▼▼▼▼▼▼▼▼▼▼▼▼▼▼▼▼▼

What Success Means to Mr. T

When you're hot, you're hot, and there is no doubt that Mr. T is the biggest new star to hit television in the past two years. One of the things that happens when you become successful in show business is that all kinds of other famous people want to meet you.

The President's wife, Nancy Reagan, invited Mr. T to the White House in December 1983, to play Santa Claus at a party for the four hundred children of the foreign diplomats who live in Washington, D.C. When it was Mrs. Reagan's turn to sit on Mr. T's knee to tell Santa what she wanted for Christmas, she planted a big kiss smack on his forehead. Mr. T was so pleased to be kissed by such an important and pretty lady that he crowed, "Wow! Burt Reynolds, eat your heart out." Everyone at the party whooped and hollered at that and you know that Mrs. Reagan was just as excited to meet Mr. T as the kids were. In fact, it was such a big deal to have Mr. T at the White House that even the President's assistants

Mr. T, playing Santa Claus, greets Mrs. Reagan at a White House Christmas party.

Mr. T's Christmas kiss from First Lady Nancy Reagan.

snuck out of their offices to get a peak at him and ask for autographs to take home to their own children.

Mrs. Reagan had invited Mr. T because he has worked just as hard as she has to keep kids off drugs, and she wanted to show her appreciation to him. "I was so honored," Mr. T said, "because the First Lady of the land recognized what I've been doing."

Before the party was over, every kid there had his picture taken with Mr. T. They all took home a Mr. T doll and had a story to tell that not one of them would ever forget.

Someone at the party asked Mr. T what gift he would have for President and Mrs. Reagan if he were the real Santa Claus. He said, "Peace and love. We need more love. We don't need more things to buy, we need to give from the heart."

Some actors complain that being famous makes it too hard to go out in public. They can never be alone and do what they want without having to stop to sign autographs or have their pictures taken. Mr. T loves the crowds of kids who swarm around him wherever he goes. The older ones want to ask questions, touch his gold chains and check out up close how big and strong he really is. The littlest ones just like to crawl onto his lap for a hug.

Nobody knows for sure except Mr. T, but people guess that he makes over three million dollars a year. Over a million dollars of that money comes from the people who pay him to star in *The A Team* and *The Mr. T Show*. He also gets about $45,000 every time he appears on any other television show. He's paid thousands and thousands more dollars when he makes a movie. Then there are the Mr. T dolls, Mr. T fake gold jewelry, Mr. T wigs and little

Kids can't resist checking out Mr. T's gold chains.

A fan checks out Mr. T's bulging biceps.

And the littlest fans just want a hug from Mr. T.

Mr. T making a muscle to match the Mr. T doll—or is it the other way around?

▼▼

trinkets like Mr. T puffy stickers and Mr. T rubber stamps. Mr. T gets paid "royalties," which are a percentage of the price, for the use of his name and picture. He's very careful about how his name and image are used, however. You can buy a Mr. T shirt or a Mr. T comic book, for example, but you'll never see Mr. T beer or Mr. T cigarettes.

But success always brings big responsibilities, for Mr. T as much as for anyone else. Mr. T has to pay his agent at least ten percent of his income, or about $300,000 a year to take care of his business affairs. The government takes away about half of the money he makes—taxes amount to around one million, five hundred thousand dollars. So Mr. T probably ends up keeping only about one million of his three million dollars.

Still, it's a long way from the "oatmeal, no meal and miss a meal" poverty of his childhood. When Mr. T was a little boy with nothing but hand-me-downs in his closet, his idea of success was "to have enough clothes to go three months and never wear the same thing twice." Nowadays he could wear a different outfit every day for a *year* if he wanted to, not to mention the hundreds of gold chains and medallions he owns, and the gold and diamond rings on every finger.

Success also brings awards. In 1984, fans voted Mr. T their "Favorite Male Performer in a New TV Program" on *The People's Choice Awards* on television. He was also named one of the Ten Most Desirable Bachelors in the World. That honor doesn't mean beans to Mr. T. Although there are plenty of women who would like to go out with him, Mr. T doesn't date. And he has no plans to marry. "There are two women in my life, my mama and my daughter," he explains.

Some other political people besides the President's wife have also honored Mr. T. When he visited New York in March 1984, Mayor Edward Koch presented

Super-singing star Lionel Ritchie with Mr. T at the People's Choice Awards. They both won top awards, voted on by fans.

Mr. T receiving the key to the city from New York Mayor Edward Koch.

Mr. T with the key to the city in a ceremony at City Hall. The very next day, Mr. T collected a second city key from Mayor Harold Washington in his own home town, Chicago.

The most important show business awards are the Emmys for television, and the Academy Awards for movies. Mr. T hasn't won either of those yet, but he's not bothered by that. "You can win ten Academy Awards, you can make a hundred movies," he says, "but if you don't have God in your life, you ain't got nothing." He doesn't care about acting awards or what the critics say about how good or bad his acting is. Mr. T believes that the people are his judge and with them, he's doing just fine, thank you.

"All I'm trying to do," he says, "is keep my feet on the ground and my head toward heaven." His family helps keep the fame and money from going to Mr. T's head. Two of his brothers work for Mr. T as bodyguards, one of his sisters is his personal secretary and other brothers and sisters go with him when he travels. "They keep me together," he says. "It's the peace. I have someone to talk to and they understand me because they watched me grow up."

Mr. T likes to do as much as he can to share his good fortune. He tries to make at least one personal appearance every week. He stops by to help cheer up kids in hospitals and he goes to nursing homes to visit old folks who can't get out and around anymore. He visits schools to talk to the kids about studying hard, not dropping out and not doing drugs. He never gets paid for any of these visits.

Once in a while, when Mr. T hears a story that especially touches his heart, he goes out of his way to do something nice. One very sick little boy wanted

Two lucky girls get autographs to take home with them.

▼▼▼▼▼▼▼▼▼▼▼▼▼▼▼▼▼▼▼▼▼▼▼▼▼▼▼▼▼▼▼▼▼

to meet Mr. T more than anything else in the world. When someone told Mr. T about him, Mr. T arranged to have the boy brought to the set of *The A Team* where he had lunch with Mr. T and the other stars of the show. Another time, Mr. T made a special trip to Council Bluffs, Iowa. Four thousand, one hundred school kids had signed an invitation that was *three hundred feet* long. A piece of paper that size would stretch about as far as one hundred seven-year-olds laid end to end.

Mr. T knows that the outward signs of success—fame, popularity, awards, money—are fun to have, but they are not important in themselves. He wears half a million dollars worth of jewelry at any one time, but if someone tried to steal it, Mr. T would just hand it over. "It's okay to have possessions," he says, "but don't become possessed by your possessions. Don't cry over something that can't cry over you." If he lost everything tomorrow, it wouldn't matter to Mr. T. He says he would thank God for the

Two superheroes. Mr. T with Olympic gold medal
winner Edwin Moses.

▼▼▼▼▼▼▼▼▼▼▼▼▼▼▼▼▼▼▼▼▼▼▼▼▼▼▼▼▼▼▼▼▼▼▼▼

time he had. "I'd still be happy. I had fun with it."

Even though he is the star of the No. 1 show on
NBC—even though he could never have time in his
whole life to shake hands with the millions of people who want to meet him—even though he makes
millions of dollars and wears pounds of gold—Mr.
T *still* doesn't think he is a star yet. He measures
success differently. He won't be a star to himself
until he does three things. One, he wants to buy his
parents a big home to make up for the years everyone in the family crammed themselves into that
teeny-tiny apartment. Two, he wants to build a community center in Chicago for the poor people in the
neighborhood where he grew up. And three, he
wants to feed five thousand people, just like Jesus
did with the fishes and the loaves. When he does
those three things, *then* Mr. T will believe in his
heart that he is really and truly a star.

"I'm trying to set an example for the young blacks

in the ghetto who have been deprived . . . I'm trying to set an example for the people who've been on welfare, who came from a broken home," he says.

A lot of people told Mr. T he would never make it, that he didn't have a chance to crawl out of the poverty of that Chicago slum. But he believed his mother when she said that if he tried, if he always did the best he could, he would grow up to be somebody. In the ways that the world measures success, Mr. T succeeded beyond his wildest childhood dreams. And by his own yardstick of success, he's getting pretty close.

Now he has another dream. He wants to be a full-time preacher, and he says that in four or five years he will give up acting and show business to do that. "I will be traveling. I won't have one church because I don't think one church can hold my ministry," he says. "See, I belong to the world."

Chapter 6

▼▼▼▼▼▼▼▼▼▼▼▼▼▼▼▼▼▼▼▼▼▼▼▼▼▼▼▼▼▼▼▼

What Mr. T Believes

"If I looked nice," Mr. T says, "it wouldn't have any effect. What I've been saying about no dope and no alcohol, I've been saying for years. But who would listen?" Mr. T has used his eye-popping size, his weird haircut, his earrings, and his glittering chains to startle people and get their attention.

"I want the people to listen when I say stay off drugs. You don't have to be robbing and looting and stealing. You don't have to be snitching anybody's purse." He wants kids to stay in school, study, and learn enough to be somebody. He wants kids to work just as hard at educating themselves as they do at sports. "That's our problem," he says, "we've got muscle-bound bodies and malnutritioned brains." He warns kids that he doesn't want them watching *The A Team* unless they've finished their homework. Mr. T repeats these things again and again at the schools, churches and community centers where he shows up to spread his message. And he backs that message with his mind-boggling strength and brawn. "I tell people they should be thankful to God that

Mr. T manicures his Mandinka. Check out Bible and cassette machine for playing back his church pastor's sermons.

what Mr. T knows is on the right side," he says. "Because just as good as I am good, I could be that much terrible bad." He tells the crowds that gather to hear him speak that he came from poverty. But if he looked for something better and found it, anyone can.

"I see myself as sort of a Pied Piper," he says. "I feel I've been called by God." Mr. T is a born-again Christian, rebaptized in 1978. He belongs to the Cosmopolitan Community Church in Chicago and

Mr. T visiting the children's ward at County-USC Medical Center in Los Angeles.

▼▼▼▼▼▼▼▼▼▼▼▼▼▼▼▼▼▼▼▼▼▼▼▼▼▼▼▼▼▼▼▼▼▼▼▼▼

he joins in the services and activities there when he can. When he is in Los Angeles, the church's pastor, Reverend Henry Hardy, sends tape cassettes of his sermons so that Mr. T can listen to them and do the Bible studies at home. His religion and his church mean so much to Mr. T that when he was interviewed by Barbara Walters, he sat with a Bible in one hand and a cassette player holding a tape of one of Reverend Hardy's sermons in the other hand.

"I don't shout on Sunday and doubt on Monday," says Mr. T. He practices his faith every day of the week. He prays every morning and night and before every meal. He is also a tither; he gives his church ten percent of all the money he makes. In Mr. T's case, that is over $300,000 a year, and he lets the Reverend Hardy decide where the money can best be used.

By living clean, loving God and working hard, Mr. T wants to set an example for everyone who will take the time to listen to him, most of all—kids. "That's the reason Mr. T doesn't do drugs. That's the reason Mr. T doesn't drink. That's the reason Mr. T doesn't carouse," he says. "If I was to do something wrong, I wouldn't be hurting just Mr. T. I would be hurting millions and millions of kids who want to be like Mr. T."

Mr. T's examples for his own life are Jesus and Dr. Martin Luther King, Jr. He says that those two men are his personal heroes and he tries to live up to their standards of behavior. From them Mr. T says he "learned to be tough and tender—to be of tough mind and tender heart at the same time." He's tough when he says, "I am not Jesus. So if you hit me, Mr. T would not turn the other cheek." But the kids he visits in hospitals know how tender Mr. T can be when he gives them rides on his big, broad shoulders, murmuring, "I love you, I love you."

Mr. T believes all his riches and success are gifts from God and he believes that God uses him as His messenger. "I'm being about the business of letting the blacks, the Puerto Ricans, the poor whites, the poor Irish, the poor Catholics know that you can make it, you know, through God, through faith."

Just like Mr. T has.

Chapter 7

▼▼▼▼▼▼▼▼▼▼▼▼▼▼▼▼▼▼▼▼▼▼▼▼▼▼▼▼▼▼▼▼▼▼

Why Mr. T Looks Like That

All that gold! Those dangling earrings! That strange haircut! What's it all for? Everything about Mr. T is a symbol, reminding him every day of what he believes in and what is most important in his life. Mr. T is a walking, talking collection of symbols from the top of his head to the tips of his toes.

He didn't always wear that strip of hair down the middle of his head. In college, older students shaved his head. It was something that all first-year football players had to go through, as a joke. Mr. T liked the look and kept shaving his head for several years. When he began bodyguarding, he saw a lot of bald-headed men around and Mr. T didn't want to look like anyone else. So he let a strip of hair grow out. Some people think his hairstyle is a Mohawk or a Mohican or even a punk cut. It's not. It is called a Mandinka, named after Mr. T's ancestors, a tribe of people who live on the west coast of Africa. "There's a proud race of people over there and I'm proud," says Mr. T.

Over half a million dollars in gold chains, medallions, rings and bracelets.

There couldn't be another man in the world who jingle-jangles about in as much jewelry as Mr. T. He bought his first gold chain in 1976. He kept adding chains over the years and now all that glitter and flash is worth over one million dollars. At any given moment, Mr. T is wearing at least half of it: fourteen ankle chains, seven earrings, ten finger rings and a minimum of one hundred necklaces. There are a bunch of medallions, charms and trinkets hanging from the neck chains, including a star of David, a

Even Mr. T takes an evening off to dance his cares away. Note taped and tattered old shoes that once belonged to his father.

▼▼▼

cross, a medal with the motto, "Try God" and a boxing glove that was a gift from Sylvester Stallone.

One of the finger rings spells out the letter "T" in sixty diamonds. A diamond bracelet says "T-N-T." "Like the dynamite," says Mr. T. "To me it means tough and tender."

All of his jewelry is made of gold. "I wear gold because I like it," Mr. T explains. "Gold represents power. And when Jesus was born, gold was one of the gifts of the three wise men. I serve a rich God."

The fact that most of his jewelry is in the form of chains is to symbolize the metal chains and shackles that bound Mr. T's ancestors when they were brought to America from Africa as slaves. "The idea is that I'm still a slave," he says, "but I'm a higher-priced slave." People ask Mr. T if that much gold isn't too heavy to wear, and he answers, "Nobody asked my ancestors if the chains got heavy around their necks."

Mr. T's feather earrings mean several different things to him. They symbolize the flight of the dove and the eagle, their power to break free of the earth's pull and aim toward the stars. He always wears seven of them, three in one ear and four in the other. Seven represents the number of times that Joshua marched around the walls of Jericho and it also reminds Mr. T of his seven brothers.

If you look closely at photographs of Mr. T, you will see that he always wears a pair of taped and tattered old boots. He wants to keep his poor and humble beginnings in mind and not let his fame give him a swelled head. His father wore those boots and so did his brothers before Mr. T grew into them. He says he could afford gold shoes now, but he won't even wear new boots until he buys his mother a mansion.

Mr. T sometimes wears clothes made of greenish-tan camouflage fabric, both on screen as B.A. Baracus and in real life. The material was invented years ago for the Army so that soldiers can blend in with the trees and leaves, making it harder for the enemy to

"...it's a jungle out there."

▲▼▲▼▲▼▲▼▲▼▲▼▲▼▲▼▲▼▲▼▲▼▲▼▲▼▲▼

see them. Mr. T wears camouflage clothes, he says with a twinkle in his eye, because, "it's a jungle out there."

His socks are usually mismatched. Mr. T says that poor kids often don't own matched socks and they are laughed at because of it. So if Mr. T wears odd socks, people can laugh at him instead—if they're brave enough, that is.

When Mr. T was on his first job at the hotel, people often called him "boy," and he didn't like that. So in 1972, he changed his name from Lawrence Tero to Mr. T. "That way," he says, "the first word out of everybody's mouth is 'Mister.'" No one, including his mother, dares call him anything but *Mister* T. "Nobody calls Muhammad Ali by his old name," he says, and anyone who tries it with Mr. T is in for "pain, lotsa pain."

Mr. T eats nothing all day on Thanksgiving and on Christmas, the two days of the year when most people stuff themselves to the eyeballs. "I fast because those days are just another day for a lot of hungry and starving people," he says. Fasting reminds Mr. T that poor people don't have enough to eat every day, not just on holidays.

There is nobody else in the world like Mr. T. "People haven't seen a man like me before," he says. "While people marvel at my size and my gold, I slip my message in on them."

His message is this: Love God, respect your parents, study hard, stay away from alcohol, don't do drugs. Be tough of mind and tender of heart. And watch out, he says, because, "There are too many dream-killers in the world. Don't let anybody tell you that you can't be somebody."

Chapter 8

▼▼▼▼▼▼▼▼▼▼▼▼▼▼▼▼▼▼▼▼▼▼▼▼▼▼▼▼▼▼▼▼▼

The Sayings of Mr. T

Mr. T never misses a chance to repeat his message wherever he goes. He has said most of these things so many times that they begin to sound like poetry. And that way, they are hard to forget. So listen up!

It's true these hands can kill. They can also heal.

I'm a sheep in wolf's clothing. I'm tough when I have to be, tender when I should be.

There are two women in my life, my mama and my daughter.

Any man who doesn't love his mama can't be no friend of mine.

I'll never make a movie that I wouldn't be proud to show my mother.

That's not acting. There's no difference between B.A. and T.

I could play Hamlet even though I look like King Kong.

The blessed of us must save the less of us.

I have been serving God since before serving God was cool.

If you don't have God in your life, you ain't got nothing.

If I didn't have God, I'd be on drugs or partying and you'd read scandals about Mr. T.

Just as good as I am good, I could be that much terrible bad.

If I was to do something wrong, I wouldn't be hurting just Mr. T. I would be hurting millions and millions of kids who want to be like Mr. T.

I don't worry. I don't doubt. I'm daring. I'm a rebel.

I am not Jesus. So if you hit me, Mr. T would not turn the other cheek.

You can't eat at the table with me if you don't bow your head and I say the blessing.

Next to God, there is no better protection than I.

All I'm trying to do is keep my feet on the ground and my head toward heaven.

Without religion I never could have become a star.

I don't shout on Sunday and doubt on Monday.

I love America! It's the only place where I could become a movie star and make all this money acting the fool.

It takes a smart man to play dumb.

Tough of mind—tender of heart.

If they didn't love me before, they can't love me now.

I'm still a slave, but I'm a higher-priced slave.

Nobody asked my ancestors if the chains got heavy around their necks.

It's not where you come from, it's where you're going.

I don't worship a governor or a mayor or the President because they are just seasonal jobs. My God was here before time was time.

Poverty made me what I am. If I had to do it all over again, I'd take it the same way.

We don't need more things to buy, we need to give from the heart.

Don't become possessed by your possessions. Don't cry over something that can't cry over you.

Do what the teachers tell you. They say, 'read,' read! They say, 'read it again,' read it again!

Study to be a scientist, study to be an astronaut. Everyone can't be Mr. T.

It doesn't take any training to be a loser.

It's easy to be a bum. It takes something special to be a winner.

That's our problem, we've got muscle-bound bodies and malnutritioned brains.

Take it from me, Mr. T.

I'd like to smell the roses along the way.

See, I belong to the world.

PHOTO CREDITS